For our wild animals

Written by: Nathan Dye
Illustrated by: Chris Dye

This is Bailey the bald eagle.
She is one of the most elegant
birds, known for being a
symbol of strength.

Bald eagle babies, known as nestlings, are solid white when they first hatch.
Here, Bailey is only a week old.

Bald eagles like Bailey are known for gracefully soaring through the air with their wide wingspans and their distinct white heads.

At 3 to 4 weeks, Bailey's feathers have gotten darker to protect her while still in the nest.

Bailey comes from a long lineage of high flyers. Her grandfather set the record for the highest single flight by a bald eagle.

They kept the trophy on the
mantle for everyone to see.

Chicks like Bailey are fully grown by 9 weeks and ready to fly at 12 weeks old.

The problem for Bailey is
that she's scared of heights.

Ever since she was a baby bird,
she was afraid to fall, so she
made her nest as close to the
ground as she could.

Bailey considers herself more of a low flyer, which sometimes gets her teased by the other eagles.

She doesn't let it bother her much,
because it's allowed her to meet some
great friends like Sterling the mouse.

One day when Bailey and Sterling were wrestling around on the ground, one of Bailey's brothers JR thought she had caught some food.

He swooped down and stole it from her...
only it wasn't food...it was her friend.

Without even thinking,
Bailey took off after JR.

She flew high and fast, chasing him and
screaming to give Sterling back.

When she finally caught JR,
she pinched him so hard
he dropped Sterling.

Bailey swooped down to catch Sterling
and they flew to safety.

When they landed, Bailey
realized heights weren't so scary
after all. From that day on, they
flew everywhere they went.

This is a story about being afraid. Sometimes our fears can be big and sometimes they can be small. Sometimes our fears can keep us from doing the things we were meant to do, but one of the best things in life is having amazing friends there to help you overcome the things that hold you back.